To the holder of this letter,

My commendations. Solving the puzzle of the chest required more than considerable deductive powers.

My work has consumed my life, and I have produced no heir to follow in my path. But I picture you: a young man of good imagination.

Any mystery devised by mortal minds can be solved therewith.

Yours faithfully,

Sherlock Holmes

OTHER YEARLING BOOKS YOU WILL ENJOY:

YEARLING BOOKS are designed especially to entertain and enlighten young people. Patricia Reilly Giff, consultant to this series, received her bachelor's degree from Marymount College and a master's degree in history from St. John's University. She holds a Professional Diploma in Reading and a Doctorate of Humane Letters from Hofstra University. She was a teacher and reading consultant for many years, and is the author of numerous books for young readers.

THE ADVENTURES OF

Shirley™

HOLMES

The Case of the Blazing Star and
The Case of the King of Hearts

by Judie Angell

A Yearling Book

Published by
Bantam Doubleday Dell Books for Young Readers
a division of
Random House, Inc.
1540 Broadway
New York, New York 10036

Created by Winklemania

Original screenplay for *The Case of the Blazing Star* by Rick Drew
Original screenplay for *The Case of the King of Hearts* by Patricia Finn

Visit us on the Web! www.randomhouse.com
Educators and librarians, for a variety of teaching tools, visit us at
www.randomhouse.com/teachers

ISBN: 0-440-41503-9

Printed in the United States of America

March 1999

10 9 8 7 6 5 4 3 2 1

OPM

THE CASE OF THE BLAZING STAR

CHAPTER

Though it was night, the moon was full and there was more than enough light for the young man to see his way around the stables. Besides, he knew the stables, the stall, and the horse so well, he could have gotten around blindfolded.

His name was Rudy Lamont, and at the moment, his best and most loving friend was standing before him: a sleek, lean chestnut racehorse with soulful eyes and white markings on her face in the shape of a kite with a tail.

Rudy began to brush the horse, softly crooning an old lullaby from his childhood.

The horse turned her head and pushed her nose against Rudy's jacket pocket.

"Oho!" Rudy said, chuckling softly. "We're starting already, are we?"

The horse nuzzled his pocket harder.

Rudy held up his hands. "Sorry, Star," he said teasingly, "I don't have what you're looking for."

1

The horse tilted her head for a moment. Then she pushed her nose against Rudy's other pocket.

"Now, where are your manners, young lady?" Rudy said, laughing. "All right, all right." He unzipped his jacket and pulled out a stick of black licorice. The horse snorted loudly. This was a favorite game both players knew well.

Rudy held the licorice to the horse's mouth, and she gobbled it quickly as he stroked her muzzle.

The two were so engrossed in their game, they didn't hear the car pull into the stable yard. The car's headlights were turned off.

"One more piece, then." Rudy held out another stick of licorice. "Y'know, you're a weird horse," he said fondly. He picked up a brush and began to groom Star's flanks.

A harsh voice spoke just outside the stall. "She was supposed to be ready."

Rudy turned slowly. "I told you, Tony," he said. "Forget it!" He went back to grooming the horse.

Tony stood at the stable door, backlit by the moon. He was tall and heavyset, with close-cropped hair. He said nothing but simply waited.

In a moment two more people joined him.

"Ms. March is here, Rudy," Tony said. "And the doc."

Rudy ignored them. He went on brushing the horse with one hand and patting her with the other.

"All right, Rudy," Ms. March said stiffly, "put down the brush."

Rudy paid no attention, but he was breathing harder.

"The last time I checked," Ms. March said through tight lips, "I was still the owner of this animal."

"Yeah." Rudy looked up at her shadowed form. "But you don't own me, Ms. March."

Ms. March eyed her two companions, who stood mute beside her. "This," she said to Rudy, "can be as simple or as difficult as you want to make it."

Rudy dropped his brush and jumped protectively in front of the chestnut horse. Ms. March nodded at Tony. Tony pulled open the stall's iron gate and moved in toward Rudy.

CHAPTER  2

Shirley Holmes was sitting on a low stone wall outside Sussex Academy, the private school she attended. Shirley was a day student at Sussex, although some kids boarded there. All the girls wore the school uniform of a white shirt and a plaid skirt. The boys wore gray trousers. Everyone wore the annoying striped tie and dark green blazer with the school crest.

Shirley's English class was being held outdoors because of the glorious sunny day, and Shirley was taking advantage of the fresh air and the pleasant smells of early fall. She brushed her long, dark brown hair back from her face and observed her classmates.

No detail escaped her curious glance. The kids sat in groups with the teacher, Ms. Goldstein, wandering among them. There was Molly Hardy, sitting on a blanket with Alicia Gianelli. Alicia was sweet and trusting, small and dark. Molly was student council president and was Alicia's opposite in appearance: tall and blond. She

4

could also be a real problem. *Never turn your back on Molly Hardy*, Shirley thought.

And there was Stink. Stirling Patterson, a pest but popular with a certain group of boys. Next to him sat Bart James, the Sussex electronics nerd.

So different, all of us, Shirley thought. *Molly and I could have been friends. What makes her the way she is?*

Shirley was every inch the great-grandniece of the legendary detective Sherlock Holmes. His portrait hung in her attic laboratory, along with his famous cape and tweed deerstalker cap.

When she was a small child exploring the attic of the Holmeses' huge Victorian mansion, she had discovered the secret of opening his ancient carved wooden file box. Inside was a handwritten letter expressing his desire for an heir to his phenomenal powers of deductive reasoning. He had assumed that heir would be male. Shirley decided that that was probably his only incorrect assumption.

Shirley brought her attention back to her teacher, who was reading aloud to the class.

" 'These trees,' " Ms. Goldstein read, " 'shall be my books / and in their barks my thoughts I'll character, / That every eye which in this forest looks / shall see thy virtue witnessed everywhere.' " She closed the book and smiled. "So, class: What better way to great allusion than here in our own natural paradise?" She bent to pick up a stack of papers.

"More like hell than paradise," Stink Patterson whispered to Bart James.

If Ms. Goldstein had heard him, she didn't acknowledge it. "I have your essays here, class," she was saying, "and by and large I was quite impressed with how inventive they were!"

Molly Hardy took hers and frowned. "An A minus?" she asked incredulously.

"I got an A!" Alicia Gianelli cried happily, and Molly glared at her.

"There must be some mistake," Molly said, and Alicia stopped smiling.

Shirley watched and nodded as Bart and Stink examined their grades.

"What'd you get?" Bart asked. He showed Stink his paper.

Stink quickly slipped his essay into his book bag. "English grades are way too subjective," he grumbled.

Bart grinned. It was a rare moment of one-upmanship for him.

Shirley was not surprised at any of her classmates' reactions. She could have predicted their grades, based on her observations of their behavior. Now she waited patiently until Ms. Goldstein reached her.

"Shirley Holmes!" Ms. Goldstein said, holding out Shirley's essay folder. "Comparing Caliban to Arnold Schwarzenegger!"

Shirley stared up at her.

"I loved it!" Ms. Goldstein exclaimed, and Shirley beamed. "Oh, and Shirley?"

"Yes?"

"Most great thinkers can't spell either," the teacher whispered, and they smiled at each other.

As Shirley watched the teacher's retreating back, she caught a glimpse of her friend Bo Sawchuk. He was sitting with his back propped against a tree, his head to one side, his eyes closed, and his mouth wide open.

Uh-oh, Shirley thought.

Ms. Goldstein was on her way toward him.

Quickly Shirley pulled the ink cartridge out of her ballpoint pen. She tore off a tiny piece of paper from a pad and stuffed it into her mouth, chewing it hard. Then she rolled the paper into a little ball and pushed it into the empty pen casing. She put the end of the casing to her lips, aimed, and blew as hard as she could.

Bo awoke with a start as the spitball hit him on the neck. He looked around and spotted Shirley, gesturing at him and pointing to their teacher. Just in time: He snapped to attention before Ms. Goldstein caught him dozing.

Ms. Goldstein stood above Bo and handed him his essay folder. "Bo—what happened?" she asked, pointing at the paper.

Bo, embarrassed, merely shrugged.

"See me after class, okay?" Ms. Goldstein said, and moved on to the next student.

Bo looked down at his paper and the grade marked on it. He slumped against the tree and folded his arms.

* * *

It was the end of the school day. Bo Sawchuk stood in front of his locker, working impatiently at the combination lock. Frustrated, he pounded a fist against the locker door.

Behind him he heard, "Seventeen left, fourteen right, twenty-two left."

Bo didn't even look up. "How'd you know?" he asked.

Shirley tilted her head. "Observation," she said simply.

Bo opened his locker and rummaged around for his books.

"So," Shirley asked, leaning against the wall, "what did Ms. Goldstein have to say?"

"Nothing."

"But you were in there for twenty minutes!"

"Yeah, so?" He still wouldn't look at her. He put on his jacket, slammed his locker, and turned to walk away.

"Where are you going?" Shirley asked, worried. Bo was a probationary student. He had once been a gang member, but, seeing his potential, the court had gotten him admitted to Sussex Academy on a special scholarship. So far he had done well.

Shirley grabbed his sleeve as he headed for the front door. "Bo, where are you going?" she repeated.

He whirled around. "Somewhere no one in this school goes!" he snapped. "To work! My parents own a fish market, remember?"

Shirley folded her arms across her chest. "Is that why you quit football?" she asked softly.

Bo frowned. "Who told you that?"

"You did."

"Huh?" He wrinkled his nose.

"Usually you come to homeroom on Mondays and Thursdays all sweaty from practice. You haven't done that for two weeks."

Bo walked away, leaving her behind.

She sniffed the air in his wake. *That's not a fish smell*, she thought.

Shirley sat on a bench in the hall and did her homework, waiting for the rest of the students to leave the building. It wouldn't take long, she knew. When the final bell of the day rang, Sussex, like most schools, cleared out fast. She glanced around. There were probably a few people left, she thought, but mostly faculty. And they would be in their classrooms.

She got up and went over to Bo's locker. It took her no more than a few seconds to open it. The smell seemed to be stronger in there.

Not the gym bag, not the books . . . wait a minute . . .

She pulled out a grimy shirt and sniffed. *This is it*, she thought. As she started to return the things to the locker shelf, something fell out of the folds of the shirt.

Shirley picked it up. It was a long piece of straw. She nodded to herself.

CHAPTER

The Sawchuk Fish Store was at the opposite end of town from Sussex Academy. Shirley rode her bike there as quickly as she could.

Bo's parents were Ukrainian immigrants, and at times it was difficult to understand them. Shirley entered the front of the store and heard their voices coming from the back room, which was used for cleaning and preparing the fish. A swinging door blocked her view into the room.

"I can't give you any more time, don't you understand?" a strange voice shouted over the broken English of the Sawchuks. "Don't even ask again! The rent is the rent!"

Shirley jumped back as a large, burly man came out of the back. He didn't notice her. "I'm not running a charity here!" he yelled back to the Sawchuks. He slapped an envelope down on the store counter, nearly bumping into Shirley as he stormed out of the shop.

Bo's mother emerged from the back room, wiping her hands on her apron. She looked distressed, but when she saw Shirley she managed a smile of greeting.

"Hello, Shirley," she said hesitantly, not knowing what the girl had overheard.

Shirley put on her happy young schoolgirl face. "Hi, Ms. Sawchuk," she said brightly. "Can I please talk to Bo?" She put her backpack down on the counter, covering the envelope the angry man had left.

"Oh . . . Bo . . ." For a moment Ms. Sawchuk looked confused. "Bo—he's at the football practice still," she said then, remembering.

Mmm—no, he's not, Shirley thought, but she said, "Football practice! Right! I'm sorry, I forgot. I guess I'll see him later."

She scooped up her backpack, taking the envelope with her.

"Goodbye, Shirley," Ms. Sawchuk said. She sounded dazed as she turned toward the back room.

Outside on the street, Shirley stopped at a parked car and rested her backpack on the hood. She took a can of hair spray from one of its pockets and sprayed, soaking the front of the envelope. The spray made the envelope transparent so that she could read some of its contents without having to open it.

There was bold lettering on the message inside: EVICTION NOTICE, it read.

Shirley took a breath. *Eviction notice* . . . The Sawchuks were going to lose their store!

11

Quickly she waved the envelope back and forth. As the hair spray evaporated, the front of the envelope returned to normal. No sign of the contents was visible.

She ducked back into the store to return the envelope and heard the Sawchuks arguing in the back.

The last thing Shirley heard as she hurriedly left was Ms. Sawchuk begging, "Please, please—try the bank again! One more time!"

Shirley's home was hidden from the road by a great lawn and large trees. She lived in the enormous house with her father, a well-known and respected diplomat, and her grandmother.

Mrs. Holmes, Gran to Shirley, loved music, painting, Chinese martial arts, and Native American sculpture. She was sitting in the kitchen, sipping tea and reading a mystery novel. At her feet, snoring, was Shirley's much-loved basset hound, Watson.

Shirley burst into the room, breathless after her quick ride home.

"Shirley, dear!" Gran said. "I'm so glad you're home. I want to start sketching you!"

"Oh, Gran—" Shirley bit her lip. She'd forgotten she'd promised Gran she'd let her sketch her portrait. "There's someplace I have to go! I'm sorry—could we please start tonight after dinner instead?"

"Ah, but we'll have lost the light," Gran said.

Shirley winked. "Don't need light for charcoal sketches, Gran," she reminded her.

Watson snorted loudly.

"You're both right!" Gran said. She smiled, scratched the dog behind his ear, and went back to her tea and book. "Off you go, then. Try not to be late, dear."

I'll try, Shirley thought as she hurried up the back stairs.

Moments later she had changed out of her school uniform and was out the door again in jeans and a cotton shirt. She fastened on her protective helmet and raced off on her bike.

On a small oval at the racetrack, the trainers were putting the horses through their paces.

Exercising horses wasn't Bo's job. His was cleaning the stalls so that they would be ready when the horses returned from their workouts.

Bo spread a mat of hay over the floor of one stall.

In the next stall a horse whinnied. She was Bo's and his friend Rudy's favorite—Blazing Star. Hearing her, Bo forgot how tired he was and opened the gate to her stall. He stroked her nose affectionately.

"Hi, Star," he said in a soothing voice. "What is it you want? *Hah!* As if I didn't know . . ."

He dug some licorice out of his pocket and offered it to the horse. But she whinnied again and turned her head away, uninterested.

"Hey," Bo said, "what's your problem? You love licorice!"

"It can't be very good for a horse's teeth," Shirley said. She was standing in the stall's open entrance.

13

Bo knew better than to be surprised at anything Shirley did, but he asked anyway: "What are you doing here? How'd you know I was here?"

She shrugged. "Simple deduction," she told him. "After I noticed the smell of horse on your shirt, I just figured—"

"What shirt?"

"The shirt in your locker," Shirley answered.

"You—You broke into my locker?" Bo asked angrily.

"Yeah," she said, hoping her attitude told him she had every right to know what was going on. "And I also went to the fish market to look for you."

"You went where?" The veins were standing out on Bo's neck.

"Don't worry," Shirley said calmly. "I covered for you. Your mom said you were at football practice and I said I'd see you later. I didn't lie—I *am* seeing you and it *is* later."

"Just hang on a minute," Bo said. "You're telling me you went through my stuff?"

Shirley ignored his comment. "So . . . Did you get a second job here to help out your parents?"

Bo was about to answer when Rudy Lamont came into the stable. He hung some tack on a post near Blazing Star's stall.

"Hey, Bo," he said in greeting. "Am I interrupting something?"

Bo was gaping at Rudy's face. "Whoa," he said. "You got a bad shiner there!"

It would have been hard to miss. The skin around Rudy's eye was black and purple. It was also puffy, nearly closing the eye.

"What happened?" Bo asked.

Rudy gave him a sheepish look. "Aw," he said, "it was my own fault." He scooped up a lead and put it on Blazing Star's halter. "I was mounting and Star whipped her head back. Nailed me a good one. Weird horse," he said as he patted her neck.

Shirley finally realized she wasn't getting an introduction, so she stepped forward. "Hi," she said to Rudy.

Bo made a face at her. "Rudy-this-is-Shirley," he said in one fast breath.

"Hi, Shirley." Rudy smiled.

"Is she your horse?" Shirley asked, nodding at Blazing Star.

Rudy had begun to lead the horse out of her stall. "Naw," he said wistfully. "I just ride her. But she's special to me. I was right there when she was born. And just about every minute of her life since then." Rudy and the horse moved slowly toward the stable door and out into the yard.

Shirley waited for the slow *clip-clop* of hooves to move out of hearing distance before she said, "Blazing Star didn't give your friend that black eye. That bruise was on the right side of his face. Horses are always mounted from the left."

Bo was still furious that Shirley had gone through his

locker. He gave her a scathing look and went back to raking the stall.

"Just observation . . . ," Shirley said. She knew Bo was waiting for her to leave, but she couldn't do that until he'd told her what she needed to know. She gathered her courage.

"Bo—your parents got an eviction notice," she said.

He stared at her for a moment, then opened his mouth and closed it again. He wanted to ask her how she knew, but it didn't really matter. Shirley found things out through investigating, and she was seldom wrong. He threw down his rake and stalked out of the stable toward the exercise track.

Shirley trailed after him and watched as he leaned against the wooden railing surrounding the track. He rested his chin on his arms.

She went to his side.

"Okay," he said at last, without turning. "I'll tell you what's going on, but on one condition: You lay off me and go home. Where you belong."

That stung, but Shirley didn't waver. "I accept your terms," she told him, "provisionally."

Bo had to smile. *"First,"* he told her, "you get on your bike."

It was leaning against the railing. Shirley straddled it and reached for her helmet, which was hanging from the handlebars. "Okay?" she said.

"Okay. Here's the deal." Bo shoved his hands into his jeans pockets. "I've got this uncle, back in Ukraine. . . .

Things are pretty tough there. My parents try to help him out. He always pays us back somehow, but . . ."

"But this time he didn't," Shirley finished.

"Yeah," Bo sighed, "this time he didn't. He couldn't."

"So you got this job at the stables to help your parents pay the rent, right?" Shirley asked.

"Yeah. Right. And they'd both totally flip out if they knew I was working here. So that's the answer to the big mystery. You satisfied? Now get lost, like you promised!"

Shirley had been listening to Bo, but she'd had her eye on the track and the people clustered around Blazing Star. Rudy was in the saddle, but Star was bucking and shaking her head, whinnying loudly.

"I thought Rudy grew up with that horse," she said. "She doesn't seem to be behaving for him."

"Would you just go?" Bo said, pointing to the front gate.

"In a minute. Who're those people?" she asked. "That woman . . . and that man with the bag?"

Bo threw up his hands. "The woman is Ms. March. She owns Blazing Star. And the guy is her vet. The horse's vet. *Now* do you know everything you have to know?"

"I guess. . . ."

"There's the gate, okay?" He pointed again. Then he turned and marched back to the stable.

Shirley began to ride toward the gate but slowed down as she heard Rudy call out to the veterinarian.

"She's real skittish!" Rudy told him.

17

But the doctor was on his way to his car. "That's to be expected," he said over his shoulder. "She'll settle down, don't worry."

Hmmm, Shirley thought, pursing her lips. She followed the doctor on her bike. He got into his car and closed the door. As he did, Shirley read the lettering painted on it: DR. NED SNODGRASS, VETERINARY SURGEON.

CHAPTER  4

The next morning at school, Shirley—on time for once—stood at her locker gathering the books she would need for first period. She heard a commotion behind her. A helium balloon was floating above a small group of laughing students. Dangling from the balloon's string was a pair of girl's underpants.

Alicia Gianelli was almost in tears as she jumped and grabbed for the underwear, squealing at Stink Patterson, clearly the cause of her dismay.

"I suppose that's probably funny on your planet!" she cried. She kept jumping, but the balloon bobbed just beyond her reach.

Stink spread his palms across his chest. "Hey, I'm as innocent as the day I was born," he proclaimed.

"That doesn't say much!" Alicia said, panting. "Get them down right now!"

The bell rang, and Stink turned away. "Can't!" he said

over his shoulder. "Gotta get to class! But don't worry—the helium'll leak out in about a week!"

Alicia screeched at him through gritted teeth. The crowd scattered.

"Aw, lighten up, Alicia," Bo said as he passed. He was tall enough to reach the balloon, and he pulled it down and handed it to her. He smiled to himself as she stormed down the hall with the balloon and underpants.

Shirley touched his shoulder. "Multiple personalities," she said.

"Huh?"

"It's the only explanation for your mood swings."

Bo grinned. "No, things are okay now. I found a way to save my parents' store!"

"Really?" They walked toward homeroom. "That's terrific! How?" Shirley asked.

"It's so cool!" Bo told her. "I'm gonna clean up on a big race this weekend!"

Shirley stopped him at the door. "You're making a bet? You're not old enough."

"It's okay. A friend's placing it for me."

"Rudy?" Shirley asked.

"No!" Bo shook his head. "Rudy's riding her. Blazing Star. The odds are twelve to one against her, but he's sure she's going to win."

"Bo Sawchuk and Shirley Holmes, will you please come into class?" the teacher called from the room.

"Um . . . we'll be right back. We have to go to Ms.

Stratmann's office first," Shirley called, dragging Bo away from the homeroom door.

"Listen, I don't need any more latenesses on my record," Bo said. "And neither do you. And nobody wants us in the headmistress's office!"

"I just need to know something."

"Duh!" Bo dropped his jaw. "Shirley, you always need to know something!"

"How is Rudy so sure Blazing Star's going to win?" she asked.

Bo sighed. "Rudy knows that horse. Really. It's a sure thing."

"Nothing's a sure thing," Shirley said. "That's why they call it gambling!"

Now Bo was angry. "Listen," he hissed at her, "why can't you just be happy for me? I'm trying to help my parents—"

"But—"

"—who don't work in an embassy and have tax-free salaries—"

"What if he's cheating?"

"—or live in big mansions!" Bo finished, and stormed back toward the classroom.

Shirley sat in the window seat in Gran's small apartment on the second floor of the Holmeses' big house. Shirley held her head up. Her hair was tied back with a pink ribbon. She looked the perfect picture of a well-bred young lady.

"Just turn your head a little," Gran was saying. "No, the other way. That's it, just right! That's exactly the way you looked last night." She was seated across the room, sketching rapidly with a stick of charcoal.

With her head turned, Shirley couldn't watch her grandmother draw, as she liked to do. Gran was still beautiful, with her snow-white hair swept back behind her ears, her blue eyes focused, and her long, slender fingers moving.

"Gran?"

"Hmmm?"

"If the odds against a horse are high, that means it's lost a lot of races?"

"That's right." Gran glanced up quickly, then down again at her pad.

"But," Shirley wondered aloud, "if the horse is that bad, why would anyone bet on him?"

"Well," Gran answered pleasantly, "the higher the risk, the greater the payoff. Some gamblers love big odds." She was silent for a moment; then she looked up at Shirley. "Think of putting down your last hundred dollars on a horse that's—oh, say, a hundred to one. And there you are, watching that horse pound down the home stretch, neck and neck with just one other! In a single stride, that horse could make you very rich! Or . . . leave you penniless. It's that very instant many people live for." She went back to sketching.

Shirley didn't share that excitement about gambling.

"Uh-huh," she said, "but if a jockey says he's sure he's gonna win, could that mean he's fixing the race?"

Gran smiled. "Usually you fix a race by deliberately losing. That clears the way for another horse to win, you see? And you bet on that horse."

Shirley frowned.

"Of course," Gran continued as she drew, "there's always steroids."

Shirley's eyes widened.

Shirley had her arms full carrying Watson, her basset hound, and had to knock at the door of Dr. Ned Snodgrass's office with the toe of her shoe.

The horse veterinarian from the stables opened the door abruptly. He had his bag in his hand and looked as if he was on his way out.

Shirley gazed up at him pleadingly. "I know you're mainly a horse doctor, but could you look at him, please?"

"Shouldn't you be in school?" the doctor snapped.

"School's out. I'm at Sussex and we get out earlier. Of course, we have to be there earlier in the morning—"

"I'm due at the track," the doctor said.

Shirley looked as if she might cry. "Oh, *please!*" she begged. "He's got some straw in his eye."

"I have no time—"

"But his eye's so red—please, please, please? His name's Watson." She thrust her armful of dog at the doctor.

The vet heaved a sigh. "Oh, all right, come in," he said. He took the dog from her and placed him on the examining table in his office. Watson yawned heartily.

Shirley positioned herself next to the doctor and began to babble. "He's a basset hound, but of course you know that, don't you, being a vet and all? I really wanted a bloodhound, but my dad said they grow too big and our yard is small. But basset hounds are fine too, they look funny when they run, did you know that Shakespeare compared them with Thessalian bulls?"

The doctor rolled his eyes, unable to concentrate with Shirley's chattering. He sighed. "Why don't you just wait out here?" he said. He hefted Watson and disappeared into another room.

Within seconds Shirley was rifling the doctor's file cabinet. She quickly located the file marked BLAZING STAR. She took her camera pen from her pocket and snapped a picture of each document in the file. She returned everything to its proper place and was pacing the room when Dr. Snodgrass returned with Watson.

"How is he?" she asked with her best look of concern.

"There's nothing wrong with this animal," the doctor said huffily. He put Watson down. "Red eyes are characteristic of the breed!"

Watson looked up sadly.

CHAPTER 5

Shirley hurried along the racetrack grounds, with Watson keeping pace on his short legs.

Suddenly the dog stopped.

"Watson?" Shirley said. "Come on, now." She gave his leash a little tug, but Watson pulled it out of her hands and took off toward the stables. Shirley followed him.

Inside the barn Bo was stacking bales of hay. Watson waddled up to him, wagging his tail.

"Hey, Watson!" Bo said with a smile. He knelt to pet the dog, then realized that if Watson was there . . . He looked up and, sure enough, there was Shirley at the stable door.

"Oh, man," Bo said. "I should have known you wouldn't keep your promise."

"I know, I know," Shirley said. "I said I'd leave you alone. But I just need to know why Rudy lied about his black eye. And why Blazing Star has been acting up."

"She hasn't." Bo jerked his head toward the horse's stall. "See? Calm as anything."

Shirley observed Bo. "Why," she asked, "is a horse that's finished last five times in a row suddenly expected to win?"

Bo looked confused. "Well, she had a bad leg," he said. "So Rudy's been holding her back. But it's healed now."

"What if he's giving her steroids?" Shirley asked with a hard stare.

"No way!" Bo kicked at a bale of hay. "No way!"

"Steroids increase aggression. That would explain why Rudy's having a hard time handling her."

There was an angry snort from the stall. Shirley looked down. Watson had left them and run off to play with Blazing Star, scooting under the stall's gate.

"Don't worry," Bo said, moving toward the stall. "Star loves dogs." As Bo reached the stall's gate, the horse suddenly reared, whinnying at the basset hound and nearly coming down on the dog.

"It's okay, girl," Bo said soothingly to the horse, trying to grab her halter. But Star continued to neigh and kick the air. Shirley was able to duck away from the horse's flailing hooves and seize Watson's leash. She kept her head down and escaped from the stall, dragging her dog behind her. Bo wasn't so lucky. Star came at him, kicking high in the air. Bo desperately backed away and found himself pinned to the wall as the horse continued her tantrum.

In the midst of the neighing and bucking, Shirley heard confused voices and footsteps just outside. In a moment she was facing Rudy, along with Ms. March and her aide, Tony. Ms. March looked stiff in a purple tailored suit and brimmed hat.

Rudy rushed into the stall and calmed the horse, leaving Bo free to make a hasty exit.

Ms. March pulled him aside. "I ought to fire you!" she shouted. "Star could have been hurt! Bringing your dog into the stables like this—"

"He's my dog," Shirley said, stepping forward.

Ms. March turned ferociously on her. "And just who are you?"

Rudy came out of the stall. "It's all right," he said. "Really, Ms. March, it's not a big deal. Star likes dogs."

Ms. March gave Rudy a significant look. He nodded slightly, and she seemed to relax a bit. She turned back to Shirley. "You," she said, "get out. If I see you around here again, I'll call Security."

Shirley ground her teeth and began walking with Watson toward the door. But she stopped, suddenly noticing something on the floor in front of Blazing Star's stall.

"And as for you—" Ms. March now turned her wrath on Bo. "I expect a day's work for a day's pay, young man!"

"Eeeuw!" Shirley cried as she stepped into a pile of horse droppings. No one paid her any attention, and she limped out of the barn.

Once outside, she went around to the side of the building and took off her soiled shoe. Watson sat patiently as she balanced on one foot and took a plastic bag out of her backpack.

"Evidence," she muttered as she began to scrape the droppings from the sole of her shoe into the bag.

"Not anymore!" Bo was beside her in an instant. He grabbed the shoe from her hand and threw it as far as he could into an open field.

"Bo, that was—"

"Stop treating me like a specimen you put under your microscope!" he shouted. A lock of his straight brown hair fell over an eye. "There's no mystery here!" he continued. "It's just my life! My life! Why can't you just leave me alone!"

Shirley felt her heart beating rapidly. Her stomach hurt. She was trying to be a friend! How could she make Bo understand?

"It—It's just that I'm worried about you," she stammered.

"Well, you've got a funny way of showing it. You almost got me killed. And then you almost got me fired!" He turned on his heel and walked away from her.

Watson was looking up at her with his sad hound's eyes. Shirley pointed to the field where Bo had thrown her shoe.

"Fetch," she said with a sigh, and the dog trotted off.

CHAPTER 6

Shirley's darkroom was in a corner of the attic out of the way of all possible light.

Now the little makeshift entrance curtain was parted and Shirley, in a white lab coat, sat at a small table. Above her, drying on a line, was an eight-by-ten photograph she had developed. It was one of the snapshots she'd taken in Dr. Snodgrass's office.

She frowned at a test tube filled with a brown liquid, then glanced over at a glass plate that showed a series of colored bands.

She looked at the bands, then back at the test tube.

Bands.

Test tube.

At last she gave up. They just didn't match.

"No steroids," she mused, bewildered.

She picked up her notebook and drew a line through that item on her checklist. "No steroids," she repeated softly. She held the beaker with more of the liquid from the test tube. There was something tiny floating in it that she hadn't noticed before.

She took a pair of tweezers and plucked the particle from the beaker. Then she examined it under a magnifying glass.

"It's an oat," she said to herself. She reached for the photograph clipped to the line above her. It was a picture of a medical form with various items listed in columns. Next to each item was a little square.

Shirley looked down the page to the column marked ALLERGIES. One of the squares had a check mark. "*Ahhh*," she murmured. Now she allowed herself a smile.

Shirley searched the track grounds until she located the locker room, where the jockeys changed from their everyday clothes into brightly colored racing silks. Shirley hoped it would be empty so that she could continue her investigation.

The only people at the track who knew her were those she'd met when she'd visited Bo in Blazing Star's stall. No one else would pay any attention to her at all. Besides, since it was race day, the entire staff was busy preparing for the events.

There was a small alleyway between the locker room and the track office. Shirley thought it might be a good place to hide, as no one seemed to be using it. She leaned against the barnwood siding and waited.

"Hey, Rudy!" she heard Bo call. "You look good!"

Shirley peered around the corner of the office and saw Bo speaking to Rudy, who was walking Blazing Star.

"Not now," Rudy said brusquely, scowling. "I gotta get ready to race."

"Great," Bo said cheerfully. " 'Cause I'm betting on you."

Shirley bit her lip.

Rudy stopped and turned. "What?" he asked.

"The race." Bo smiled, bragging, "I'm putting all I got on you."

Rudy shook his head and sighed. He was obviously upset.

"There's no risk," Bo said. "You said yourself that—"

Rudy gave Bo a hard look, annoyed. "I don't think it's such a good idea. What would your parents think?"

Star kicked a hoof at the ground and refused to walk any farther. Bo looked at her. "What's wrong with you, anyway?" he asked the horse. He looked back at Rudy. "I don't know who's crankier lately, you or Star."

Rudy softened his look and gave Bo a pat on the shoulder. "Hey, you're learning," he said. "Try to feel what she's feeling. Be nice to her. She's got a race to run." He handed Star's lead rope to Bo and walked off. Bo led Star back to her stall.

Shirley kept her eyes on the door to the locker room, watching as the jockeys crossed the alleyway on their way to the starting gate.

When they had all left, she made her way into the

locker room and looked around. She needed a disguise so that she'd look as if she belonged at the track. Someone had left on a hook a windbreaker and a jockey's helmet with goggles. Shirley slipped them on.

They were slightly too large for her, but it didn't really matter. Most jockeys were small, and Shirley was small too and was now wearing a costume that would allow her access to all areas of the track without being noticed.

She left the locker room and turned toward the stables. She immediately saw Ms. March and Tony approaching. Shirley pulled her goggles over her eyes and confidently strode past them.

Blazing Star was alone in her stall. Shirley knew Bo would be there shortly and he'd be angry with her again, but there was something she had to find out.

She opened the stall door gingerly. This was the horse she'd previously seen in a frenzy, so she began to murmur soothing words as she approached.

Blazing Star was covered with a light blanket. Shirley carefully lifted it away.

"I know you have a tattoo somewhere saying who you are," she whispered. "If I could just find it . . ." She parted the horse's mane, found nothing, then lifted Star's tail.

The horse stamped her hooves, and Shirley jumped. "Easy, girl," she crooned.

Blazing Star flicked her tail out of Shirley's hand, and Shirley drew back. From her pocket she took a small bottle and a cotton ball.

"What do you think you're doing?" Bo stood at the door, glaring at her, but Shirley continued her work. She opened the bottle and dabbed some of the liquid onto the cotton ball.

"It won't hurt her," she said. "It's potassium iodide." She rubbed the cotton ball on Blazing Star's forehead.

"Listen, Shirley, that's a hundred-thousand-dollar horse," Bo told her, but then he stopped speaking, stunned as the white star on the horse's forehead turned reddish brown.

Shirley noted Bo's openmouthed gaze. "Her star was put on with bleach," she explained.

"No way!"

"She's not the real Blazing Star," Shirley told Bo. She knew how hurt he would be by this news. But there was just no other explanation, and Bo had to know. "Rudy switched horses."

Bo's impulse was to be angry, but he stopped himself. Suddenly it all made sense to him. "This horse hates licorice and doesn't like dogs. And she doesn't like me," he said.

Shirley nodded. "It all began to make sense when I found oats in this horse's droppings. According to her medical records, the real Blazing Star is allergic to oats."

"That's right," Bo agreed.

"There's one more thing to check," Shirley said.

"What?"

"Her registration tattoo."

Bo nodded. "That's what you were looking for."

"Uh-huh."

Bo felt confused and powerless. He didn't know how or whether to answer her. "Look, Shirley, what are you gonna do if it *is* the wrong horse? Huh? What I mean is, I know what you'll do, but are you going to report it before or after the race?"

"You placed your bet," Shirley said. It wasn't a question.

"Everything I've earned," he told her.

Shirley sighed.

"It isn't just the money," Bo said. "I've known Rudy for five years! He taught at a camp I once went to. There's no way he'd do something like this."

Shirley said nothing.

Bo balled his hands into fists. He looked at the ceiling, then at the floor. *If only . . .* , he thought. *If only . . .*

"The tattoo's on her lip," he said finally. He reached for the halter and pulled the horse's head down. "It's here."

"What's going on?" Rudy, in green-and-white silks, stood at the stable door. He was holding an empty canvas bag.

Shirley stepped out of the stall, and Rudy looked her up and down. "That looks like Roy's jacket," he said. "What are you doing here, anyway? You heard Ms. March. I should call Security."

But Rudy's manner suggested that he had other things on his mind. He went over to a large trunk between two stalls, reached into it, and pulled out a horse brush and other grooming equipment. He put the things into the canvas bag, then reached for a saddle that was hanging from a hook on a post.

Shirley glanced at Bo. He nodded. "Go," he told her. "It's okay."

Shirley hesitated but realized Bo needed to talk to his friend alone. She started to leave, then spotted something black sticking out of Rudy's pocket. Licorice, she realized.

She left the stable and waited by the door for Bo. She could still hear Bo and Rudy inside.

"Listen, Bo, you can't bring your friends around here anymore. You know that. This horse belongs to Ms. March, and she has the right to—"

"Which horse, Rudy?" Bo didn't even wait for Rudy to answer. "I can't believe you'd ditch Blazing Star! After all your talk about generosity and treating a horse the way you'd treat a friend."

"It isn't what you think," Rudy said, ashamed.

"Where's the real Blazing Star?" Bo demanded.

"Look, kid, the less you know, the better. You gotta trust me on this," Rudy said.

"I did trust you," Bo declared. "And I'm not a kid! I'm calling the cops!"

Shirley ducked around the corner as Bo came out of the stable. *At least Rudy didn't hurt him,* she thought. *Rudy doesn't seem to like what's going on with the horses any more than Bo does.*

She noticed a horse trailer on the far side of a paddock

and quickly made her way to it. She checked over her shoulder—no one in sight—and stepped into the trailer.

Peering around, she saw the hindquarters of a chestnut horse. It was wearing a saddle identical to the one Rudy was going to put on the horse in the stable. She inched her way along the mare's body. As she reached the horse's head, the horse turned and nuzzled Shirley's neck. There on the horse's forehead was a kite-shaped white mark.

"Blazing Star," Shirley said with a smile. "I knew you couldn't be too far away from Rudy."

Shirley heard a man's voice outside the trailer. "I'll get her," the voice said. It was Tony. He opened the trailer door and immediately spotted Shirley. An angry look spread across his face, and he climbed into the trailer and started toward her.

Shirley dodged around the side of Blazing Star and jumped past Tony and out of the trailer. As she turned to run, she collided with Ms. March.

"You!" Ms. March grabbed Shirley by the shoulder and held her tight.

Tony jumped out of the trailer and took hold of Shirley himself.

"Do something with her!" Ms. March ordered.

CHAPTER

"And . . . they're off!"

Shirley could hear the track announcer, then the bell signaling the start of the race. She sat hidden behind a stack of hay bales in the stable loft. Her hands were tied behind her back at the wrists, and her mouth was taped shut.

Outside, the announcer called the race. "Wicked Widow takes an early lead!" He spoke excitedly into the microphone. "Here comes Paula's Pride up on the inside! And moving through the pack is Blazing Star!"

Shirley rolled onto her back, brought her knees tight against her chest, and managed to loop her feet under her bound wrists so that she could then bring her hands in front of her face.

She lifted her wrists to her face and pulled off the tape with her fingers. Once her mouth was free, she used her teeth to untie the knot at her wrists.

"Blazing Star is gaining ground," the announcer

shouted over the crowd's cheering. "And coming round the bend, it's Whistler's Mudder, grabbing the lead from Paula's Pride."

Shirley shook herself free of the ropes.

"Look out for Blazing Star, coming up the middle!" the announcer yelled. The crowd's cheers grew wilder.

Shirley headed for the open trapdoor in the loft and peered down. There was no ladder, and it was a long way to the floor.

Shirley eyed the hay bales. If she dropped them through the trapdoor to the ground, she could build up a platform to land on.

The bales were heavy. Shirley pushed against one and inched it over to the trapdoor. As she pushed it through, she lost control and stumbled, falling through after it. Desperately she reached out and grabbed for the edge of the trapdoor opening. "Help!" she cried.

Bo came into the stable and looked up, astounded to see his friend hanging high above the floor.

"What are you doing here?" he asked.

"It's a long story," Shirley said, tightening her grip. "Bo, I'm slipping."

"Hang on!" Bo shouted, and frantically began to pile hay bales under her dangling feet. "Just hang on!"

"As they close on the finish line, it's Blazing Star and Whistler's Mudder!" the announcer yelled.

"Bo!" Shirley called. Her knuckles were white from gripping the edge of the trapdoor opening. She slipped, lost her grip, and fell. She let out a scream.

Bo had just tossed another hay bale onto the pile and was directly under her. She landed right on top of him.

"And it's Blazing Star at the finish line! Followed by Whistler's Mudder and Paula's Pride!"

Shirley immediately rolled off Bo. "Are you okay?" she asked worriedly, but she could see he wasn't badly hurt. There had been enough hay to cushion both of them. Bo sat up and rubbed his shoulder.

Shirley stood, brushing herself off. "You broke my fall," she told Bo gratefully.

"I broke . . . something," he said, then smiled. He pushed himself to his feet. "C'mon," he said, and they both rushed for the door.

They pushed their way through a throng of onlookers at the winner's circle. There was a proud and red-faced Rudy, holding Blazing Star's reins. A blanket of flowers hung around her neck.

"They won!" Bo said happily. His face was shining.

"Look over there," Shirley said, pointing. Tony and Ms. March were being escorted to a police car.

"You called the police?" Shirley asked.

"Not me. Rudy," Bo answered.

"Ahh." Shirley nodded. "Let's go see him."

They waited until all the photos had been snapped and the congratulations were winding down. Rudy was feeding the horse a treat.

"You rode the *real* Blazing Star," Shirley said to him.

"How'd you know that?" Bo asked.

"The licorice in your pocket."

39

Rudy laughed and scratched the horse's ears affectionately. "Weird horse," he said, chuckling.

"You planned to ride her all along, didn't you?" she asked.

Rudy nodded. "Well, Ms. March and Tony wanted me to put her back in her stall after the impostor horse won, in case there were questions. Bo and I just made the switch a little early."

"Ms. March thought Blazing Star was washed up after her tendonitis last year," Bo said. He looked up at the horse fondly. "But Rudy had faith in you all along, didn't he, girl?"

"And you had faith in Rudy," Shirley said.

Bo grinned at her. "Shirley Holmes, are you admitting you were wrong?"

Shirley stiffened. "The word *wrong* connotes a certain—"

"She's hopeless!" Bo interrupted, slapping his thigh. "You can't even admit it!"

CHAPTER  8

Shirley stood at the edge of the football field, waiting. When the play was finished, a heap of boys in practice uniforms lay in a pile on the field. One by one they pulled themselves off each other until only one boy was left on the ground: Bo.

It took a moment for him to rise, but when he did, he was grinning. He held up his prize—the football—and the coach blew the whistle.

"Okay, ladies!" the coach shouted. "Hit the showers!"

Shirley walked over to Bo. "Does it feel good being back on the team?" she asked.

"Mostly," he said, and rubbed his shoulder.

"So, what exactly did your parents say when you told them how you got the money?" she asked.

Bo grinned. "Well, first they said, 'Thank you.' "

"And second?"

Bo shook his head and smiled. "Second—um, except for football, I'm grounded for life."

Shirley laughed and gave her friend a pat on the back.

THE CASE OF THE KING OF HEARTS

CHAPTER  1

Stirling Patterson, better known to his classmates as Stink, kept his head down and peered through his blond bangs, scanning the cafeteria. Lunchtime was the usual at Sussex Academy: low-level talking, the clattering of utensils. Even the lunch was the usual—fish fillet sandwiches and fries.

From under his chair, Stink pulled a small bottle of white vinegar. He poured it into his empty water glass.

Shirley Holmes, sitting at another table with Bo Sawchuk, glanced over just as Stink put the vinegar bottle back under his chair. Shirley noted Stink's sly expression, as did Alicia Gianelli and several other students. Though they hadn't caught him in the act, he looked suspicious, and everyone knew that when Stink looked suspicious, a prank was on its way.

Stink got up from his table and went over and tapped Alicia on the shoulder. "Hey, Alicia, want a sip?" He offered his glass.

Alicia looked from his keen eyes to the glass. It looked like water, but she guessed it wasn't. "Yeah, right," she answered with a curl of her lip.

"Aw, come on," Stink urged. "It'll make your hair shiny!"

"Hey, Stink!" said a voice behind him.

Stink turned quickly, nearly spilling the liquid.

Bart James came over to him, an angry look on his reddened face. "You were supposed to help me clean up the science lab!" Bart complained. "I had to do it alone! Thanks a lot!"

"Aw." Stink shrugged amiably. "I totally forgot. Hey, I'm sorry. You must be thirsty from all that work. Here." He pushed the glass toward Bart.

"Yeah, well . . . ," Bart said, calming down. "Thanks."

Shirley and Bo watched as they ate their lunches.

"He's taking it," Bo whispered.

"Mmm, what a surprise," Shirley said, and sighed. "Like a lamb to the slaughter. Every time."

Bart was about to drink, with half the cafeteria population's eyes on him, when Ms. Stratmann, the headmistress, hurried toward them. Bart and Stink cringed.

"Mr. James, Mr. Patterson." Ms. Stratmann was panting. "I had to find you both. I just came from the science lab and—"

"Ms. Stratmann, I didn't—" Stink interrupted, but Ms. Stratmann wouldn't be put off.

"—it just looks splendid!" she finished. "Excellent work!"

Stink glanced at Bart, who scowled back at him.

Ms. Stratmann was still smiling. "You both did such a wonderful—Oh . . ." She broke off and began to cough.

All talk in the cafeteria abruptly stopped as Ms. Stratmann turned away from the boys and continued to cough into her cupped hands.

"Are you okay?" Stink asked.

Ms. Stratmann's eyes watered. "Something . . . in my . . . throat . . ." She began to pat her chest and took a handkerchief from her pocket.

Bart thrust forward the glass Stink had given him. "Here!" he told her. "Drink this!"

"No!" Stink cried, but it was too late.

Ms. Stratmann gratefully grabbed the glass from Bart and took a large gulp.

"Oh, no," Shirley said under her breath.

Stink rolled his eyes to the ceiling. "I'm doomed," he mumbled.

Ms. Stratmann emitted a great choking gag as she spewed forth a mouthful of vinegar. The students all stared at her contorted face and Stink's look of terror.

"Vinegar!" Ms. Stratmann cried.

"What?" Bart cried. He grabbed the glass from the headmistress and sniffed it. "It *is* vinegar!" He glared at Stink, who was busy trying to think of an excuse, while Ms. Stratmann dabbed at her lips with her hankie.

Stink could only wait in horrified silence until Ms. Stratmann recovered.

"Oh!" Ms. Stratmann finally said, balling up the handkerchief in her fist. "Why, I . . ." She let out a laugh and then smiled. "I expect that was your idea, Mr. Patterson," she said. She let out another loud laugh.

Stink's mouth opened and closed. He was speechless. Everyone in the cafeteria was stunned that Ms. Stratmann thought the prank was funny.

Ms. Stratmann kept laughing. She patted Stink on the shoulder and walked away, still chuckling to herself. She picked up a rolled poster on one of the tables, moved to the cafeteria door, and taped the poster to the glass panel in the door. She stepped back to admire the poster, which announced a special Roman history class, then let out another guffaw and swept out of the room.

The stunned silence in the cafeteria remained. Even after Ms. Stratmann had left, it took a moment for the babbling to start up again.

"Did you *see*—?"

"There was vinegar in that glass."

"Stink did it."

"I know it wasn't Bart."

"Yes, but did you *see*? Stratmann was *laughing*!"

Alicia Gianelli gaped at Molly Hardy. "You know, I started kindergarten at Sussex, and in all this time I don't think I've *ever* seen Ms. Stratmann laugh!"

Molly was relatively new to the school, but even she

knew that the headmistress rarely smiled and *never* laughed.

"I mean, not even a giggle!" Alicia exclaimed.

Bo stared at Shirley, confused. Shirley didn't get what was up with Ms. Stratmann either.

CHAPTER  2

The next day at lunchtime, the students filed into the cafeteria. Stink's prank and Ms. Stratmann's coughing fit were forgotten, thanks to the students' collective embarrassment: They were all wearing Roman "togas," made from white bedsheets held together with safety pins and draped over their school uniforms. Even the teachers were costumed like ancient Romans.

White papier-mâché architectural columns had been placed around the room. Grape leaves made of crepe paper had been strung from the ceiling. The doorways and windows were masked with painted cardboard to resemble Roman arches.

Ms. Stratmann presided over the party, swirling about the room in her own white toga. "Welcome, *all*, to our Roman banquet!" she exclaimed, greeting the students.

Stink frowned. "Hey, you think it was the vinegar?" he asked Bart.

"Maybe it's not really her," Bart said, still staring at

the headmistress. "What if she's the victim of a body snatching?"

Arthur Howie, a stately-looking history teacher with a clipped white beard, stood near the refreshments table in extreme discomfort, his toga draped over his shirt and tie and a fake crown of grape leaves on his balding head.

Ms. Stratmann approached him and made a great sweeping gesture with her arms. "Hail, Arturius Howie!" she proclaimed loudly, and then whispered, "See what I mean about making history come alive?"

He returned a weak smile as she breezed off.

"Interesting look for you, Mr. Howie," Shirley noted. She was standing at his elbow, nibbling grapes.

"*Et tu*, Ms. Holmes?" he replied with a withering glance, and moved away.

Whoa, what'd I say? Shirley wondered.

Ms. Stratmann was clearly the only one in the room who was enjoying herself. As the students stood around feeling silly in their togas, she offered them plates of figs, stuffed grape leaves, and brightly colored sorbets. She held a plate out to Bo and Alicia.

"Don't just *stand* there," she exhorted. "*Immerse* yourselves in the splendor of ancient Rome!"

Alicia took a fig from a plate and frowned.

"Alicia, you must learn to savor every experience!" Ms. Stratmann said with a sigh. Alicia gingerly nibbled the fig. The headmistress drifted away, appearing as light as the fabric of her toga.

Shirley joined Bo and Alicia, as bewildered as they were at their headmistress's oddly cheerful behavior.

"Maybe she got a new car," Bo said.

"Maybe she won the lottery," Alicia offered.

"Maybe she's sick," Shirley said worriedly.

"Mmm, yeah, maybe," Bo mumbled, and then someone pushed his shoulder. "Hey!" he complained.

Molly Hardy glanced at him haughtily over her shoulder as she passed the little group. "Sorry," she said brusquely. "I've got a job to do."

Molly had been Shirley's nemesis since Molly had come to Sussex for the fall semester. They watched each other warily whenever their paths crossed. They could hardly have been more different. Shirley was smallish, with long dark brown hair; Molly was tall with blond hair and a snotty tilt to her slender neck. Shirley was quite aware of the way Molly had used trickery to win election to the office of student council president. She knew Molly had cheated, but she hadn't been able to prove it. Molly Hardy was still the darling of the administration.

"Ms. Stratmann?" Molly tapped the headmistress on the shoulder.

Ms. Stratmann turned. "Molly," she said sweetly. "Isn't this wonderful, this 'living history'?"

Molly had little interest in ancient Rome. She held out a file and a pen to Ms. Stratmann. "I need your signature on this document now, because if we don't—"

"Molly, Molly! Business can wait. Please. Enjoy yourself." Ms. Stratmann gestured toward the refreshments

52

table. "Go have some dates Alexandrine!" She turned with a big smile toward a group of boys. "Have you boys tried the dates Alexandrine?"

Molly clicked her tongue and started to follow the headmistress. "Ms. Stratmann, being student council president, I have responsibilities that—"

"Well, well, if it isn't Molly Hardy . . ."

Molly turned at the sound of the gruff voice behind her. Her jaw dropped. A sour-looking man with a fat mustache and a stiff, soldierlike manner stood before her. She gulped and tried not to show her surprise.

"What are you doing here?" she asked the man.

He gave her a cold stare. "You'll find out soon enough," he said menacingly. "And this time, I'll be ready for you." He looked away from Molly. "Ms. Stratmann," he called.

Ms. Stratmann flitted across the room to him. "Bob Kemp!" she cried enthusiastically.

Mr. Kemp held out his arms, grandly waving to the room. "A veritable Roman holiday, I see," he said, smiling a tight smile.

"Come, I'll give you a toga! Oh!" Ms. Stratmann blushed. "I mean, a tour! Come along."

Mr. Kemp followed Ms. Stratmann, taking a small black book out of his pocket as they moved around the room.

Shirley narrowed her eyes at Molly. It wasn't often she caught Molly looking genuinely upset.

"Who was that?" Alicia asked Molly.

"My old principal," Molly muttered glumly. "He was . . . *let go*."

Shirley noted Molly's annoyed look. "You got him fired, didn't you?" she asked.

Molly tossed her head. "I may have . . . *influenced* the decision," she replied.

"What's he doing here?" Bo asked.

Molly's expression became one of fear. "Looking for a new job," she guessed.

They all turned to stare at Mr. Kemp. His piercing eyes surveyed the room as he busily wrote notes in his black book.

"But we already have a headmistress," Alicia said.

Suddenly Shirley got it. She gave a little gasp. "Stratmann's leaving!" she exclaimed. She tugged at Bo's sleeve and pulled him toward the door.

Bo and Shirley sat in the school's library. It was dark and quiet. Everyone was still at the Roman banquet. Only a small reading lamp shined on their table above the medical textbook they were examining. Shirley stabbed her finger at a particular entry.

"Hypomania!" she cried. "I'm positive this is it! Listen: 'A gradual onset over a ten-to-fourteen-day period. The patient appears physically normal, but out of character.'"

Bo quickly leaned over to read. "'Behavior lacks the usual social restraints . . . elated moods lead to faulty judgment . . .'"

He was interrupted as the door was flung open and Ms.

Stratmann came in, followed by Mr. Kemp. They didn't notice Shirley and Bo in the far corner.

"And of course," Ms. Stratmann announced with a grand gesture, "the library reading room!"

"Impressive," Mr. Kemp noted with a nod.

"Actually," Ms. Stratmann said, swishing her toga, "I find it a little *r*epressive! It really is . . . too *quiet*!"

Bo jumped, startled, and the adults noticed them hunched over their books. Ms. Stratmann tossed them a light wave and exited laughing. Mr. Kemp pointed at Bo. "Tighten that tie, young man!" he barked before turning to follow Ms. Stratmann.

Bo quickly pulled at his tie, even though no one was watching anymore. Shirley returned to her reading.

"There must be a treatment," she said, running her finger down a page.

Bo still had Mr. Kemp on his mind. "What if it's terminal?" he asked, worried. "I mean, for *us*?"

CHAPTER

The next day was Saturday. It was early fall, but on the chilly side, and Shirley and Bo wore jackets and scarves. Shirley had a gray knit cap pulled down over her ears. They huddled behind a massive oak tree on a residential street, watching Ms. Stratmann's house, their eyes fixed on the FOR SALE sign on the front lawn.

"We can't let her quit," Shirley told Bo. "She's obviously too sick to realize what she's giving up."

"Yeah," Bo agreed. "What else has she got besides Sussex Academy? I think she was planted there when it opened."

They were staring at the house so intently that they hadn't even heard the bicycle pull up on the street behind them.

"Bird-watching, you two?" a snide voice asked.

Shirley and Bo whirled around to see Molly Hardy on her bike with a camera hanging around her neck.

Shirley gave her a suspicious look.

"What are *you* doing here?" Bo asked Molly.

Shirley lifted her chin and answered Bo. "Molly has her own perverse reasons for wanting Ms. Stratmann to stay." She looked at Molly. "If Mr. Kemp becomes the headmaster, it's 'game over' for you," she told her.

Molly flicked her hair back with her fingers. "Please," she said with a sneer, "the *game* is only over when *I* say it's over."

Suddenly there was a sound from the house. Molly quickly laid her bike down at the curb and ducked behind a bush near Shirley and Bo.

The three classmates watched as Ms. Stratmann left her house on the arm of a tall, broad-shouldered man with salt-and-pepper hair and a matching trimmed beard. He wore a leather windbreaker and dapper white scarf. Ms. Stratmann was wearing a red plaid wool jacket, instead of her usual dark coat. Her hair was loose and flowing, and her cheeks were as red as her jacket. As they walked briskly down the path to the street, she clutched the tall man's arm tightly. She smiled at him and tilted her head against his shoulder.

Bo clapped a gloved hand over his mouth. He was laughing. *"Hypomania!"* he chortled. " 'A gradual onset over a ten-to-fourteen-day period'—oh, man!"

Shirley frowned at him. "What?" she asked.

Bo shook his head, still smiling. This particular branch of knowledge did not occupy a slot in Shirley's scientific mind. "Shirley, she's leaving Sussex 'cause she's got a *guy!*" he explained.

Molly was giggling too, though her mind had already begun to whirl with schemes. "Yeah, she's got a guy," she said. "An *old* guy, but a guy!"

Shirley turned her curious gaze toward Ms. Stratmann and her "guy" as they headed toward the nearby park, holding hands. "Come on," she said to Bo.

Without a glance toward Molly, they moved off toward the park.

The "lovebirds" were gazing into each other's eyes.

" 'And the sunlight clasps the earth. And the moonbeams kiss the sea . . . ,' " the man was saying.

"Oh, Brian," Ms. Stratmann sighed.

Shirley and Bo peered at them from behind a bush.

"She doesn't usually smile like that," Shirley said. "You know—with so many of her teeth showing."

Molly rode by on her bike, stopped, and snapped a picture of some pigeons.

Bo nudged Shirley. "What's she up to?"

"I wish I knew," Shirley answered. She could never be sure that Molly wasn't up to some no-good scheme.

They looked back at their headmistress.

The man Ms. Stratmann had called Brian was still reciting poetry.

" 'What is all this sweet work worth / If thou kiss not me?' " he finished.

"I love Shelley," Ms. Stratmann sighed.

"And I love you," Brian said, lifting her chin.

"I'm gonna puke," Bo said, rolling his eyes.

* * *

Moments later Shirley and Bo were tracking Ms. Stratmann and Brian as they continued their stroll through the park.

Brian picked a glowing autumn leaf from a maple tree and handed it to Ms. Stratmann, who tucked it into her hair and smiled at him.

"No sign of Molly," Shirley remarked, looking around.

Suddenly a small boy in a bright blue down jacket and ski cap came running up to Brian. He was clearly upset, near tears.

"*Daddy!*" he cried, tugging at Brian's sleeve. "Where have you been? Mom's crying and the baby's sick!"

Brian drew his arm away and took a step back. "Who the devil are you!" he exclaimed.

The boy desperately grabbed at him. "Daddy—you have to come home!"

Brian glowered. "I'm not your daddy!" he cried.

"Please, Daddy, please!" the boy begged.

Watching them, Ms. Stratmann looked shell-shocked. Then she pulled herself together. "Brian," she said, "it looks like you're needed elsewhere." She stalked off toward the street. "Taxi!" she shouted, waving her arm.

"Cynthia, wait!" Brian called as he hurried to follow her.

But Shirley was watching the boy. "Quick," she told Bo, "you follow Brian! I'm going after that little kid!"

It wasn't hard to follow the electric blue of the boy's

jacket, and he didn't go too far. Right up ahead, near a small, crowded refreshments stand, Shirley watched the boy hold out a mittened hand to Molly Hardy, who smiled at him and handed over a crisp five-dollar bill.

Shirley whipped out her pen camera and snapped a picture of the payoff. As the boy disappeared into the crowd, Molly glanced up and met Shirley's eyes. She smiled wickedly.

Shirley remained stone-faced. Molly had paid that boy to make Ms. Stratmann believe Brian was married. *And* had two children. Shirley took a deep breath. *All right, Molly*, she thought. *The game is on.*

Behind her she could hear Ms. Stratmann still trying to hail a taxi. Bo was sticking close to the couple; he had cleverly found a rake and had begun to gather leaves, pretending to be a park employee. Shirley hurried over and picked up the burlap sack at his feet. She bent down and pushed the leaves into the bag as she and Bo carefully moved closer to Ms. Stratmann and Brian. Shirley and Bo hid their faces as they tried to catch every word the couple exchanged.

A taxi pulled up to the curb, and Brian held Ms. Stratmann back. "I tell you, Cynthia, I've never seen that boy in my life!"

Ms. Stratmann straightened her shoulders and tried to maintain her dignity. "Brian, that boy called you Daddy," she said.

Shirley could hear the deep hurt in the headmistress's voice.

"I haven't got any children! You know that!" Brian protested.

Ms. Stratmann looked directly into his eyes. "That's the point," she said. "How much do I *really* know about you?"

He sighed. "The only children I've ever had are other people's: spoiled rich kids who sneer at the stuffy professor who thinks art and literature are important."

Ms. Stratmann didn't speak as she considered his explanation.

Shirley and Bo continued to work with the rake and sack while keeping a discreet but close watch on the pair.

Ms. Stratmann shook her head. "This is all happening so fast, Brian . . . I just feel so—out of control."

Brian took her by the shoulders. "Cynthia, believe in your feelings. Believe in *me*!" he begged.

Bo raked some leaves toward the bag but missed its opening entirely. He could almost feel how badly Ms. Stratmann wanted to believe that Brian was telling the truth.

Brian held Ms. Stratmann's shoulders tightly. "Don't you see, it was just some sick joke! Kids today, they're just . . ." He turned away. "I just don't fit into this world," he said sadly. "I'm old-fashioned. A nineteenth-century man in a cold, modern age . . ."

"Where *nothing* makes sense," Ms. Stratmann agreed, her voice soft.

Brian quickly turned back to her. "Darling," he implored, "I've shared my dream with you. Only you! To have a school in the Third World—a chance to teach underprivileged children. After all these years, I'm so close! Don't give up on me now."

Ms. Stratmann shook her head, "Oh, Brian, you'll find another teacher. . . ."

"But I want more than a teacher, Cynthia!" he cried, gazing into her eyes. "I want . . . a *wife*."

She looked back at him adoringly, all her anxiety melting away.

" 'Grow old along with me!' " Brian said, quoting another poem. " 'The best is yet to be.' "

"Browning," Ms. Stratmann sighed. Brian knew all her favorite poets.

The taxi waited at the curb. She moved toward it, but before she could open the door, Brian pulled her toward him and kissed her. He let her go and she climbed into the cab.

"I can't live without you," he told her through the open window.

She touched her lips where he'd kissed them as the taxi pulled away.

CHAPTER

Once Ms. Stratmann had gone off in the taxi, Brian slowly grinned a wide, evil grin. He pulled a handkerchief out of his pocket and wiped Ms. Stratmann's kiss from his face. He strolled away, whistling softly to himself.

"Did you see that?" Shirley whispered to Bo.

"Yeah," Bo said, nodding. "He doesn't look like he's so in love now that Ms. Stratmann's out of his sight."

"That's for sure," Shirley agreed. They followed Brian as he approached an outdoor cafe and sat down at a table where a beautiful young woman was already seated, tapping her foot impatiently.

Shirley noticed that there were no waiters, but a young man in a greasy apron was working as a busboy, wiping the tables. When he went inside the cafe, Shirley grabbed an extra apron off a hook by the door and slipped it over her head. She picked up a napkin dispenser, attached a tiny microphone to its side, and casually made her way over to where Brian and the woman sat.

" I almost lost her," Brian told the woman. "This stupid kid came up to us and called me Daddy!"

"What?"

"Some weird joke, I guess. Anyway, sweetface, I pulled it right out of the toilet and we're back on track." He gave her hand a light squeeze.

The woman smiled at him.

Shirley placed the napkin dispenser on the table between Brian and his "sweetface," then quickly made her way back from the table. She hung the apron on its hook by the door and retreated from the cafe.

Hidden from the couple by some bushes, Shirley and Bo watched and listened carefully to Shirley's tape recorder and receiver as they picked up the signal from the microphone.

"Old Mother Hubbard," Brian said, chortling, "she went to the cupboard. And guess what it was filled with? *Money!"*

The woman laughed with him.

"Judith, when Cynthia sells that house, there'll be at least a quarter million there!"

"That's more than we got from that blonde in Brentwood," Judith replied.

"Yes, but remember the twins?" Brian asked. "We sure got them for a bundle."

"You're good," Judith said with admiration.

Brian leaned toward her over folded arms. "Without

either one knowing, both sisters in my arms handing me over their inheritance," he bragged. "And after they found out, they were too embarrassed to press charges."

"You have no scruples," Judith said gleefully.

"Hey," Brian said. "They got what they paid for." He held out his arms expansively. "Me—the man of their dreams!"

Shirley shook her head. "More like their nightmares," she remarked.

"Listen, Judith," Brian said, "I had to propose to her to keep her hooked, so let's get ready to route the money through the offshore account."

"He's gonna rip Stratmann off!" Bo whispered to Shirley.

"Seems to be the plan," Shirley agreed.

Bo frowned, "I mean, okay, so she gives a lot of detentions. But, jeez, she doesn't deserve this! What're we gonna do?"

"We have to warn her," Shirley answered.

"How?" Bo asked.

Shirley looked back at him. She didn't have a clue.

From a distance Molly Hardy watched the scene at the refreshments stand. The man, a woman . . . and Shirley Holmes and Bo Sawchuk listening in through a receiver. Molly knew she had to come up with a plan of her own.

CHAPTER

Shirley's grandmother sat propped up in bed, reading, in the small apartment she occupied in the Holmes mansion. The apartment was a warm, snug, safe place filled with everything that was "Gran": an easel, oil paints, stone sculptures, artifacts from around the world, tons of books.

Shirley, in a colorful kimono, stuck her head through Gran's bedroom door. "Gran, how do you explain a perfectly normal, sensible person suddenly falling madly in love?" she asked.

Gran put her book down. "The sensible ones often fall the hardest." She leaned back on her pillow. "I'll never forget the look on your very sensible father's face the night he met your mother."

Shirley continued, "Well, but what if you found out the person had fallen for a cold-hearted liar? You should tell the person, right? You should tell her, right?"

"Not necessarily. Even treacherous love must run its

course. If you interfere, the shock could destroy the very person you want to help."

Shirley frowned, puzzled.

She went down to the kitchen to do some thinking and make herself some toast for an evening snack. Her backpack was sitting on a kitchen chair. She went over and removed her small tape recorder, planning to listen to Brian and Judith at the cafe again. Then the doorbell rang, and before Shirley could answer it, it rang again and again. Shirley went to the front hall and opened the door.

A young boy in a cap stood there, grinning at her. He held up a huge, colorful lollipop.

"My dad's making me give these away to advertise his new store," the boy said. He held the lollipop out to her.

Completely bewildered, Shirley took the lollipop. A note taped to it read SUCKER.

Hmmm, Shirley thought. *Is this describing the candy or . . .* She looked at the boy and the thought hit her. She ripped the cap off the boy's head. He was the kid from the park Molly had paid to be Brian's son. Shirley glared at the boy, and he ran off.

Shirley gasped. "Molly!" she exclaimed. She rushed back into the kitchen. Her backpack lay on the floor, and the back kitchen door was open. Her tape recorder lay next to the backpack, open and empty.

"The tape!" she cried.

CHAPTER

Monday morning, Molly was at her desk in her dorm room at Sussex Academy. Shirley and Bo found her putting a bouquet of flowers in a vase of water. An open box of chocolates sat next to the vase.

Shirley didn't mince words. "You can't give Ms. Stratmann that tape, Molly," she said.

Molly held up the flowers. "These were sitting outside Ms. Stratmann's door this morning," she said calmly. "The candy, too. Lucky I was there."

Shirley folded her arms. "If Ms. Stratmann finds out Brian's a con man, it's going to push her over the edge."

"Don't be ridiculous," Molly answered, arranging the flowers. "She's tough as a yak. Want a chocolate?"

Bo reached for one, but Shirley's fierce look stopped him.

"She's not herself, Molly," Shirley said. "Apparently, love does that. And you could just drive her away more quickly."

Molly glanced up for a moment, then shook her head. "I know what I'm doing," she said.

"Really?" Bo asked. He reached into his pocket. "I wonder what Ms. Stratmann would say if she saw *this*." He held up Shirley's photo of Molly paying off the boy in the blue jacket.

Molly looked at it and frowned, but she didn't seem fazed. "Probably the same thing she'd say if she saw *this*." From her desk drawer she pulled out the tape she had stolen the night before, as well as her own photo of Bo and Shirley watching Ms. Stratmann and Brian in the park. "I'd say we have a standoff."

Shirley sighed. "Look, we both want the same thing: to break up this romance. You don't want Mr. Kemp to be headmaster, and I don't want to see Ms. Stratmann get hurt. The bottom line is Brian goes away, right? I say we make a deal."

Molly chewed her lip while she thought. "Okay," she said, "here it is: You've got three days. If you haven't changed Ms. Stratmann's mind about leaving, then I do it *my* way." She picked up her photographs and put them in a manila envelope. She began to prepare a seal, using hot wax.

While Molly worked, Shirley picked up a small card peeking out from the green paper that had been wrapped around the flowers. A playing card, she noted. A face card: the king of hearts. She quickly jammed it into her blazer pocket.

Molly was busy sealing the envelope. She had her own

monogrammed brass seal, and she pushed it into the hot wax, leaving an imprint of an elaborate M. She held it up for Bo and Shirley, to make sure they got the message. "It's secured," she said. "For three days."

After their last class, Shirley and Bo walked toward Ms. Stratmann's office.

"Remember what your gran said," Bo warned.

"Don't worry, I know what to do," Shirley told him. "My plan is to use Ms. Stratmann's naturally suspicious nature to subtly arouse her doubts about Brian."

"But the shock could destroy her," Bo replied.

They had reached the office door. "You wait out here," Shirley said. "I'll make sure she'll be spared any pain." Bo shook his head and walked down the hall. Shirley knocked at the office door.

"Shirley, Shirley, Shirley!" Ms. Stratmann sighed, with a sympathetic smile.

Shirley was disconcerted. This discussion wasn't going at all the way she'd planned. And Ms. Stratmann wasn't even calling her Ms. Holmes!

"My dear," Ms. Stratmann went on, "when we open ourselves to love, we open ourselves to life!"

Shirley cleared her throat. "But, Ms. Stratmann, don't you think my friend should be worried about her boyfriend's background? I mean, she doesn't know anything about him."

Ms. Stratmann gave her a knowing glance. "Your

'friend,' " she said in a softer tone, "should learn to trust her instincts. Trusting isn't easy, but for those willing to take the risk, the rewards are—*incredible*."

"But he'll break her heart," Shirley explained.

"Shirley, Bo won't break your heart," Ms. Stratmann said. She leaned back in her chair.

"Bo?" Shirley was dumbstruck.

"Shirley, I know you and Bo are from different backgrounds. But that shouldn't be a barrier to . . . *friendship*. Although I do think it's premature to want more than that just yet. There's a whole world of people out there to meet."

As Shirley sat with her mouth agape, a sudden *ding* sounded from Ms. Stratmann's computer. "You've . . . got . . . mail," said the computer's disembodied voice.

Ms. Stratmann watched the monitor delightedly. "Why," she said, "there's all of *cyberspace!*"

Her face flushed, Shirley left the headmistress's office. Bo was waiting for her down the hall.

"What's the matter?" he asked, trying to keep up as she strode away. "Your face is all red. You didn't blow it, did you?"

Shirley couldn't look at him.

Molly immediately emerged from around the corner and gave Shirley a sly grin.

Shirley glared back. She could tell that Molly had been listening at Ms. Stratmann's door and had heard everything.

CHAPTER

Shirley and Bo, side by side, peered at Shirley's computer screen. Bo had eaten yet another dinner at the Holmeses', and now they were upstairs in Shirley's attic laboratory.

Carefully they scrolled through name after name on the chat lines.

"Ms. Stratmann mentioned cyberspace," Shirley mumbled absently. "Maybe that's where she met him."

"There must be a million chat lines," Bo said in frustration.

Shirley handed Bo the playing card she had taken from the flowers that had been sent to Ms. Stratmann. "This is the only other lead we have. Brian's calling card."

Bo looked at it. "The king of hearts?" he asked. He took a breath and thought. "Uh . . . the poker chat line? Bridge? Old Maid?" he asked.

"Aha!" Shirley cried. "Mother Goose!"

"How do you figure that?" Brian asked.

Shirley turned toward him. "Remember? He talked about Old Mother Hubbard's cupboard with that lady at the park."

"Ohhh!" Bo slapped at the table. "*That* king of hearts! He's into nursery rhymes."

"We need a computer name from Mother Goose," Shirley said. She started to type.

Bo read the name and barked a laugh. "Contrary Mary? Perfect."

"Time to lay out the bait," Shirley said.

"Hi," Bo began to dictate. "I'm an old and desperate—"

Shirley cut him off. "Mature and established," she typed, then paused while she thought. ". . . real estate executive."

"What if he's out hustling someone and isn't online now?" Bo asked.

"Oh, he'll check in. That's how he finds his prey," Shirley answered.

After some time, Bo dozed off in an overstuffed chair. Shirley stayed at the computer and did math equations in her head to keep herself awake. Suddenly there was a *ding*.

Shirley jumped and called to Bo. "Contact!" she cried. "Bo, listen to this! 'Mistress Mary, quite contrary, if you've got space for a smiling new face, I could be the man of your dreams.' It's signed 'The Farmer in the Dell!' "

"Great," Bo said sleepily. "Some farmer guy . . ."

"Bo," Shirley insisted. "He's 'the man of your dreams'!"

Bo rolled out of the chair and leaned over the computer. "Okay," he said, "answer him."

"What do I say?"

"You know," Bo said, shrugging. "Flirt with him."

She looked blank.

"Quick. We'll lose him," Bo urged.

Shirley began to type: "What do you think of recent theories regarding quantum similarities—"

Bo quickly pulled her hands from the keyboard. "You can't send *that*!" he said. "We'll lose him for sure! You have to write something to keep him interested in you."

Shirley felt completely powerless.

"We need help," she told Bo.

CHAPTER

The next morning, as the students at Sussex Academy were pulling books from their lockers, the announcement bell sounded over the public-address system. Everyone stopped and listened to Ms. Stratmann's voice.

". . . And so I will be leaving Sussex Academy earlier than I had originally planned. Mr. Kemp will take over for the rest of the year."

Molly looked over at Shirley from across the hall. As Ms. Stratmann spoke, Mr. Kemp patrolled the halls, passing between Shirley and Molly. He paused at Molly's locker and gave her a tight smile before moving on.

". . . I hope," Ms. Stratmann continued, "that you will all wish me and my fiancé happiness in our new life together. Thank you."

Molly moved angrily to Shirley. "Clock's ticking, Mistress Mary," she hissed.

* * *

That night Shirley and Bo went again to the attic. This time they brought a pile of romance magazines and advice books with them. They skimmed the books hastily, picking up one and dropping another.

Shirley was completely confused by what she was reading. " 'Are you more attracted to sensible people or imaginative people?' " she read from the book.

"Neither. No—both," Bo answered, baffled.

" 'Are you more firm than gentle or more gentle than firm?' "

"Shirley," Bo protested. He scowled at the magazine he held in his hand. " 'Five Ways to Lose Five Pounds,' " he read. " 'Three Ways to Pretty Up that Attic Room.' "

"This is too weird," Shirley said, shaking her head.

"How about this?" Bo asked. He picked up a book and read the title. " 'Ten Ways to Make Him Care'?"

They grinned at each other. "Bingo!" Shirley cried.

They had tacked sticky-notes to the computer screen, each with a different key word to keep in mind while they wrote: *humor, confidence, honesty,* and other nouns. Shirley typed, and Bo coached.

"You certainly have a delightful sense of humor," Shirley typed. She added aloud, "For a larcenist. Don't worry, I won't type that last part."

"Shirley, you gotta pretend you *like* him," Bo urged. "Write, 'I just love to laugh, too. Hahaha . . .' Use the happy-face sign."

Shirley made a face at him but typed what he'd said and sent it off to "The Farmer in the Dell."

They read the response as it appeared on the screen: "You might say laughing is a hobby of mine."

"What baloney!" Shirley observed. "If he has any real hobbies, he should list them." She typed: "Please list your hobbies."

"Move over!" Bo pushed her aside and took over the keyboard. "Mine is golf," he typed.

The answer on the screen: "I love golf!"

Bo grinned. "He's a golfer!" He typed back: "I'm just wild about the game!"

"*Wild?*" Shirley asked skeptically.

"What's wrong with *wild?*" Bo asked.

"It just sounds a little eager," she answered.

That worried Bo. "You mean *cheap?*"

"Uh-oh," Shirley said, watching the screen. "Someone else is logging on."

"Mmm, we've got a visitor," Bo agreed.

"It's 'Little Miss Muffet,' " Shirley said. She looked over at Bo. "She wants him to paint her toenails!"

"Now, *that's* cheap!" Bo said.

Shirley peered once more at the words on the screen and abruptly clicked the Shutdown button.

"Hey!" Bo complained. "What did you do that for? It was going great! I think he *liked* us! We weren't cheap. We were direct. Honest." He tapped the *honesty* sticky-note.

But Shirley was lost in thought.

CHAPTER  9

At the end of the last class period the next day, Shirley and Molly arrived at their lockers at the same time. They looked over their shoulders at each other as students passed between them. Molly glanced away, but Shirley walked the short distance across the corridor and confronted her nemesis.

"Get off the line, Molly," she said.

"I don't know what you're talking about," Molly said, gathering up her books.

"Yes, you do, 'Little Miss Muffet.'"

Molly shoved her books under one arm and tapped her watch with her finger. "Six hours," she said menacingly, "*Mary.*"

Shirley watched Molly head for the door and join Alicia Gianelli and some other girls. They all strolled toward the dorm. Shirley turned in the opposite direction.

As she walked down the hall, she looked up and saw Brian heading toward Ms. Stratmann's office. He was smiling and carrying a single red rose. He didn't bother to knock but strode in through the open door, bent down, and kissed Ms. Stratmann on the forehead.

Shirley saw Ms. Stratmann's face light up at the surprise. Shirley moved against the wall, out of sight, and listened.

". . . I'll have the overseas funds by next week," Brian was saying. "I hate asking you for this, but it's just a short-term loan to get the work started on the building."

"Isn't it lucky my house sold so quickly!" Ms. Stratmann replied. "I don't usually have this kind of money."

Shirley winced, worried for her headmistress.

"Here, use my pen, darling," Brian said.

Oh, no! Shirley thought. *Don't write him a check! Don't give him any money, Ms. Stratmann!*

But there was nothing she could do. She hurried away to find Bo.

Shirley found Bo in the hall and dragged him toward the school door.

"What's up?" he asked.

"Brian's here with Stratmann now," she explained. "But he'll be going back to his place now that he's gotten what he wanted from her." She began walking off in another direction.

"So where are *you* going?" Bo asked.

"Miss Muffet's about to meet a Molly-eating spider!" was Shirley's puzzling reply. She headed off toward the Sussex dorm.

* * *

The fire alarm was on the wall just inside the front door of the dorm, inside a glass frame. Shirley could hear girls laughing and talking in their rooms and on the landings, but there was no one in the downstairs hall. She reached for the bright red handle of the alarm and pulled it down with a jerk. The bell rang loudly and continuously.

After a moment footsteps sounded as the students hurried downstairs for the "drill." Shirley ducked around a corner and watched everyone leave, including Molly, who looked thoroughly annoyed.

As soon as everyone had passed her to assemble on the lawn, Shirley raced upstairs to Molly's room.

Bo was at the computer when Shirley hurried into the attic room. She swung her backpack to the floor and looked over his shoulder.

"How's it going?" she asked.

Bo kept his eyes on the screen. "A little stomach-churning at times, but pretty good. No sign of Miss Muffet," he answered.

"Really! Guess she must be offline." Shirley smiled, thinking of what Molly must be doing right that minute.

Molly stood in front of her computer, furiously watching it download data. She was completely helpless to stop it from churning out its information as it tied up her computer line.

"Somebody's e-mailing me the *Bible*!" she screamed.

Back in the attic, Shirley put something down on the computer desk in front of Bo. He looked up and grinned. It was a brass seal imprinted with the letter M.

"Okay," Shirley said. "Now it's *our* game. Tell the king of hearts that you've just closed the biggest deal of your career and ask if he'd like to meet for a little celebration. *Tonight*."

Bo began to type. "Sounds great," he said, "but have you figured out which one of us is going to play a sixty-six-year-old real estate agent who's wild about golf?"

Gran was sitting in her comfortable chair, her slippered feet propped up on a soft footstool. She was reading a book when Shirley came in carrying a mug of tea.

"Just the way you like it," Shirley said. She set the mug down on the side table and leaned forward. "Gran, are you free tonight?"

"Like a bird," Gran replied.

"Well, then, how would you feel about meeting a con man for dinner?" Shirley asked.

Shirley had no worries about Molly Hardy's interference as she, Bo, and Gran got ready for the evening ahead. Shirley knew exactly what Molly was going to do, and she smiled inwardly at the thought.

* * *

In her room at the dorm, Molly picked up a photograph of herself. She removed an ornate key from the back of the photo's metal frame. The key opened one of her desk drawers, which had a secret panel underneath. From behind the panel Molly retrieved the sealed envelope in which she had stashed the pictures of Bo and Shirley spying on Ms. Stratmann and the tape she had stolen from Shirley's kitchen.

Molly hurried out of the dorm and crossed the campus to the main building, where Ms. Stratmann was packing up her office, preparing to leave.

CHAPTER 10

It was a lovely little cafe, decorated like an English pub. At one of the tables for two, Gran Holmes and Brian smiled at each other and clinked glasses.

Gran had dressed in a pale blue wool suit and a cream-colored, high-necked silk blouse. Brian, his distinguished-looking beard freshly clipped, wore a gray turtleneck sweater, a sports jacket, and slacks. He acted the part of a business tycoon, snapping his fingers and speaking rapidly. Gran stifled a yawn as he kept talking.

"So! I dropped three hundred thou into that baby, but I knew the market was soft and I had the guts to wait it out!" Brian sat back and clasped his hands behind his head.

"You clever thing!" Gran said, batting her eyelashes. "And then?"

"Whammo!" Brian said, laughing. "Through the roof! I flipped it, subdivided, and reinvested in a condo in Arizona. Say, did you mention you golfed?"

Gran raised her eyebrows. "I must have," she said.

Behind her, at a pastry cart, stood Shirley, wearing a crisp white shirt and black bow tie, black pants, and an apron. She was playing her busgirl part again as she kept an eye on her grandmother and her date. On the underside of their table, she had duct-taped her recorder, and Bo was seated at another table with the receiver. All Shirley had to do was wait for Gran's cue to move in.

Molly sat in the visitor's chair in Ms. Stratmann's office while the headmistress continued to pack her belongings into cardboard boxes.

"What do you need, Molly, some last-minute advice? It's rather late," Ms. Stratmann said as she emptied another drawer.

"Actually, I have something for you to hear, Ms. Stratmann."

"To hear?"

"Please understand," Molly said, "that I have only your best interests at heart." She put the audiotape into her machine and clicked it shut.

"Sounds ominous," Ms. Stratmann said.

Molly pushed the Play button. Suddenly the office was filled with the merry sound of an organ-grinder playing "Pop Goes the Weasel."

"Sounds cute," Ms. Stratmann remarked, and went back to her packing.

Perplexed, Molly hit Stop.

"And what about this?" Ms. Stratmann asked. She

lifted the envelope, broke the seal, and removed the photos. As she drew them out, Molly immediately realized that they were Shirley's pictures of *her*, paying off the little boy in the park! She snatched them out of Ms. Stratmann's hand before the headmistress had time to see what they were. Molly immediately tore the photos into tiny pieces.

Ms. Stratmann watched Molly, shocked by her behavior.

Molly was furious with Shirley Holmes.

Back at the cafe, Gran was sipping her cranberry tea while Brian stirred sugar into his coffee.

"So tell me about this real estate deal of yours," Brian said. "How many units did you say were involved?"

Gran smiled. "I didn't," she said.

"Ah . . . have I tired you?"

From under the table, Gran heard the tiny click of the tape as it ran out. It was the sound she had been waiting for.

She reached down and took the recorder from where it had been taped under the table. "No, Brian, or whoever you are," she said, "I'm just terribly, terribly bored." She placed the recorder on the table.

Shirley left the pastry cart and came over to the table, carrying a silver tray with a cover.

"What's going on?" Brian asked, narrowing his eyes. "Who *are* you?"

Gran didn't answer. Shirley lifted the tray's cover and

revealed another tape. She put the new tape in the player and clicked Play.

Brian's taped voice played from the recorder. *"Listen, Judith,"* it said, *"I had to propose to her to keep her hooked, so let's get ready to route the money through the offshore account."*

Gran pushed the Stop button. Shirley put her hands on her grandmother's shoulders.

Brian just sat and stared at the machine. Then he spread his arms and smiled. "Okay," he said. They'd caught him and he knew it. Now he just had to figure out a way to trick them and get away. He laughed, "Hey, I'm a lover, not a swindler," he told Shirley and her grandmother. "They gave all their money to me voluntarily. And believe me, they all got their money's worth!"

"Really?" Gran asked. "And did the government? Did *they* get their money's worth? Look over there." She pointed to a table.

Bo turned around in his chair and held up a tape and an envelope.

"That envelope," Gran continued, "is addressed to the Internal Revenue Service. The tape is a copy of the one we just played for you." She smiled warmly. "Feel up to a little jail time for tax evasion?"

Brian tried to hide his anger, but his eyes gave him away. "What do you want me to do?" he asked through clenched teeth.

Shirley leaned over him. "Tell Ms. Stratmann your school fell through. Tell her you're going abroad to recover from your disappointment. Fortunately, you haven't cashed her check yet, so you can give it back to her." She grinned. "Along with a dozen red roses!"

Brian's neck was purple, and a small vein throbbed at his temple.

CHAPTER  II

Ms. Stratmann walked slowly toward Sussex Academy's main building. She looked thoughtful, but not bereft. In her hand she carried a single red rose, which she pressed to her lips.

"Ms. Stratmann!"

She turned and saw Mr. Howie, the history teacher, the tails of his coat flapping as he hurried toward her.

"Hello, Arthur."

"Uh . . . First of all, I'd like to tell you how—uh—glad we are that you're staying on after all."

"Thank you."

"And . . ."

"Yes?"

Mr. Howie cleared his throat. "Ms. Stratmann, about your plan to turn the school swimming pool into a Roman bath. After due consideration, I . . ." He wiped his mouth with a handkerchief. "I have to tell you that I feel the idea is rather . . . ill-conceived." Nervously he cleared his throat again.

"I agree," Ms. Stratmann said, nodding.

"You *do*?"

"It was a momentary weakness on my part," the head-mistress said wistfully. "Please forgive me."

"Uh—of course!" Mr. Howie said, nonplussed. "Of course." He walked off, shaking his head.

"But, Arthur?" Ms. Stratmann called after him.

"Yes?"

"I do think we should try the Roman banquet again next year, don't you?" There was a small sparkle in Ms. Stratmann's eye.

Mr. Howie forced himself to smile and nodded, although inside he was unhappy at the thought of having to attend another toga party.

Shirley and Bo watched this scene from behind a huge oak tree, shared a smile, and began to stroll to class.

Shirley took out her journal and made some notes as they walked. *Of all the mysteries I've investigated,* she wrote, *love is the most perplexing. What makes rational, intelligent people willingly relinquish their sanity? It beats me, but one thing's for sure.*

They had reached the building, and Bo opened the door for Shirley. She gave him a surprised smile at his gentlemanly gesture, then dropped her head and concentrated on her writing.

It's never going to happen to me, she wrote.